# Our Secret 2



The Sacred Secret is exposed to…, what next?

(Mother and Son's Secret)

## Karena Donger

# Table of Contents


OUR SECRET 2 ...............................................................................1

CONTENT WARNING .....................................................................4

FREE BONUS ..................................................................................5

OUR SECRET IS EXPOSED ............................................................7

FREE BONUS ................................................................................31

ABOUT THE AUTHOR ................................................................33

OTHER BOOKS ............................................................................34

# Content Warning

This book is solely for people who are over the age of legal adulthood due to its sexual content. There are themes with a lot of bad words. All characters are well over the age of eighteen.

*It's time to stop calling you "squirt," She remarked. I prefer the name "Alpha - Gusher."*

**--Tasha**

# Free Bonus

**Grab My "At The Beach (Erotic Romance Story)" Ebook For FREE!**

Today you can grab your copy of my Free Erotic Romance story e-book titled – **At The Beach**. Best of all, it won't cost you a thing.

*Download and Subscribe for Free book, giveaways, and new releases by* **Karena Donger.**

Click the image above to **Download the Book**, and also Subscribe for Free books, giveaways, and new releases by me.

Or Follow the link below;

https://mayobook.com/karenadonger

As my subscriber, you will enjoy more free books exclusive to subscribers only, plus **Free Giveaways**. Wait no further, join my growing number of book lovers, and let's connect.

# Our Secret is Exposed

A displeased Aunt Tasha was watching Joel from the kitchen door as he was getting his mother sexy and having her fucked so hard.

However, he was not pleased to know that his mother's sister was present to watch him drive a cock into his mother. He didn't know what she was going to do after the incident. He was concerned, deeply.

It was only then that he whispered,

*"What if she tells someone?"* to his mother.

The concern in Joel's voice told Ellen that his heart wasn't in the fucking anymore, but she was too busy bouncing up and down on his stiff rod to speak.

She grunted so that Tasha could hear her.

*"She doesn't dare tell anyone,"* she said.

The fastest divorce you've ever seen will happen if she does.

If she does, I have a tape that her husband will get.

Tasha pressed the issue, saying;

*"You said you destroyed that tape. Didn't you?"*

*"I lied."* Ellen said.

It's no secret that my husband has an interest in *voyeurism*. He likes to match the dog's style to your actions on the video-tape. True to his nature, I believe he would prefer to hump you if there were no repercussions for doing so.

She called her *"sick"* for claiming that her brother-in-law fucked her after he fucked his son. What extortion!

Joel inquired, *"What's on the tape?"*

*"Your virtuous aunt is having sex with her husband's brother-in-law."*

Tasha retorted,

*"He wasn't my brother-in-law back then, and I was*

*drunk.*"

If you fucked your husband's brother the night before your wedding, I don't think your husband would accept that as a justification.

On the night of a big party, my sister and her voyeur husband were parked in a nearby parking lot, taking pictures of the area.


Ellen, on the other hand, was preoccupied with her son's rod, her clit twitching, and the rising fluid in her belly, as she rode up and down the red flesh.

Joel's crotch was pressing against her uterus, and she had no idea what else to do with herself.

She'd never been so stuffed with a man's flesh before.

Every woman's desire was to have a husband like hers, but she couldn't help but love her husband. She had the option to fuck him or not at any time.

Tasha; seeing her sister take part in such a taboo act only fueled the fire that was already raging within her.

Joel, please, please do it. Push it in. Give your entire cock to Mom. I'm going to cum again, baby.

I'm going to cum again. "

There was an exclamation of "*Ohhhhhhh Joeeel!*"

As she raised her feet and let all of her weight fall on Joel's lap, she drove his cock as far into her pussy as it was humanly possible to go, with a mournful cry.

Joel's enormous head was drenched in her fluid, which cascaded down his torso and onto his genitalia.

The fantastic orgasm that was coursing through her made her stop breathing for a brief moment before she snapped her head back against his shoulder and opened her mouth wide to take in the huge gulps of air that she desperately needed.

A hula dancer's ass kept on moving for the duration of her performance.

 She suddenly froze to the point of death. It was as if she had been subjected to a brutal beating. It was finally time for her dry, raspy voice to be heard.

*"Oh Joel, that was the most amazing fuck I've ever had in my life. Anytime, not just now. "*

Ellen leaned in and kissed him on the lips as she twisted on his lap.

Her tongue slid between his lips and became entwined with his own. He made her pussy twitch with his cock.

She leaned into his ear and said,

*"I sensed that you haven't cum yet, have you, my son?"*

Joel shrugged his shoulders.

Ellen leaned in and kissed him on the ear.

*Tasha, why don't you fuck?*


*"No problem, and she'll never be able to tell anyone you fucked her."* said Ellen to Joel.

*"How, and would she accept it?"* Joel asked.

"You can command her to do anything you want, but she will never disobey you because she has a fear of authority. It's just one of her oddities. Act as if you're in charge. If you try it, you'll see for yourself." – **Ellen** replied.


It took Ellen a while to get her feet back on the ground and slowly lift herself out of the enormous shaft.

The thought of fucking her son once more briefly

crossed her mind, but she decided to wait until they had Tasha completely under their thumbs.

With her legs splayed wide in front of her son, Ellen slumped into the back cushions of the settee.

Joel's red-headed cock stood throbbing in the air as Ellen made her way toward the couch.

For the first time, Joel had a clear view of his mother's wet pussy. With each passing moment, the desire to bury his huge cock in that tight pussy becomes stronger.

Tasha was still in the doorway, staring at her nephew's enormous cock, and he gazed at her.

In Joel's stern voice, he ordered Tasha to join him.

Her expression was one of astonishment. *"What?"*

Joel repeated, *"I said, come over here."*

Tasha made her way across the room slowly and came to a halt next to him. His weaving wand, which he held in his crotch, caught her attention instead of his face.

A rapid increase in respiration caused Tasha's large breasts to expand.

This young woman had a slim figure with wide hips and nicely formed thighs. Her attire for the day was a short denim skirt and a white shirt.

Joel beckoned his aunt, *"Tasha,"* to come closer. She didn't move until he said it a second time.

Tasha came within a few feet of him and sat down.

*"Pull up your skirt a notch,"* I said.

*"Joel!"* Tasha shrugged her shoulders.

*"Please, Aunt Tasha, don't make me ask you the same questions more than once. What did I tell you to do? "*

Her gaze never leaving his, she carefully raised the hem of her skirt till he could see her white pantyhose at the crotch.

"*Pull up further,*" he ordered her.

Tasha rolled her eyes, but continued to raise the skirt.

Her entire pussy mound was now visible. A tell-tale damp spot could be seen where the material vanished between her legs.

A gentle touch from Joel's hand to stroke his cock made him more rigid and ready to bang his aunt.

He told her to "*pull off your pants now.*"

Tasha said, "*Joel, nooooo,*" but her gaze was firmly fixed on his cocked grin. Lipped with saliva, she sat up straighter.


"*Aunt Tasha, are you having any trouble hearing me?*"

"*Oh Joel,*" said Tasha.

Hooking her fingers into the waistband, Tasha pulled her underwear down to her calf and slid the panties down.

As she lowered her hands, her skirt fell.

Her pantie-falling legs dipped to her ankles, revealing her bare ankles. She pushed the panties aside with her toe as she stepped out of them.

*"Okay, now you can raise your skirt,"* said Joel.

For the first time, Joel saw the swollen lips of Tasha's lightly hair-covered mound as she slowly emerged from the shadows.

In response, Joel pointed to the ceiling, and she raised her skirt higher, until she was exposed nearly to her waist.

Joel reached out and ran his finger along the moist slit, from bottom to top.

Tasha sighed and said, "*Oh, god.*"

*"Move closer to me."* Joel ordered her.

When Tasha got close enough to his hip, he pushed her back away.

In order to get a better look at her, Joel removed the two buttons from her shirt and lifted it over her head.

Tasha's heart raced, but she remained silent. Her tits resembled two cones. She was wearing a thin bra, which showed off her hard nipples.

Joel instructed her to remove her bra.

Because he required her to follow his orders, it was not in his best interest to remove them himself.

She closed her eyes and unhooked the straps on her back. The bra slid down her arms to her wrists as she extended her arms forward. She threw it on the ground and opened her eyes wide enough to see him face-to-face.

Joel was in disbelief at the events that had transpired. Now his stunning Aunt Tasha stood naked in front of him, as fresh as the day, after he had just fucked his mother.

Tasha tits were perfectly cone-shaped, something he'd only seen in magazines before.

He was close to shooting himself in the face in his rage. His crotch hardened.

The head was red-purple and swollen to a size he had never seen before, with ridges evident all the way down its length. He had a big hard-on, and Tasha gasped at the size of it.

*"Tasha, sit on my lap like my mother did."* Joel instructed her.

*"She was doing it to you. But, I can't. She was sitting on your... your... your."* Tasha said.

*"Aunt Tasha, I was fucking her just like I'm going to fuck you."*

*"No, no no. You will not fuck me. I'm your aunt, and it's against the law to fuck a close relative. "*

Inbreeding, on the other hand, isn't a good thing because it could lead to the development of undesirable traits. I recall you telling Mom that you couldn't get pregnant because you were on a new birth control pill.

"As a result, what's stopping us from getting a little fuck now? " Joel concluded.

Tasha uttered an agonized *"Ahhhhhhhhhhhhhh."*

Then her gaze shifted to his quivering manhood, which was protruding from his crotch.

Again, she licked her lips to dryness. She felt a squirm in her pussy. She had no doubt that he was going to insert that huge cock into her at this point.

Her juices were gushing out of her pussy holes. She'd

be dripping in a matter of seconds.

Her well-curved ass was cupped in Joel's right-hand side with his right hand. Her right leg was being drawn over his legs as he tightened her against him.

Tasha was surprised to find herself perched atop his monster dick.

With his right hand, Joel pressed down on the back of her head. As he lowered her right leg, he kissed her passionately on the lips.

When she opened her leg, she felt the head of his enormous cock gracing her pussy lips.

She pressed her lips to his and moaned. With his fingers on her ass again, Joel hauled her up into his lap and slouched down next to her. As he lowered her, her thighs clung to the outsides of his legs, causing her to slowly descend.

*"Joel, my goodness. What are you doing to me, God? "*

Tasha super-sized pussy lips was heavily stretched as Joel's huge and monster cock entered Tasha's flooded, wet pussy.

*Ohhhh... Arrrrghhhhh… Huhhhh…… She screamed!*

She trembled with fear.

During the orgasm, her scream rang out through the house. The first of many orgasms that she will remember for the rest of her life.

It was as though the weight of her head was squeezing through his aunt's narrow snout.

Even though she squeezed him so tightly, her hot oily fluid kept the passageway slippery, allowing him to glide until his cocked head was resting deep inside her juicy pussy.

She could not imagine it.

*Joel fucked her mercilessly.*

Joel increased the pace of the strokes he was giving to his aunt.

*She moaned heavily as he was fucking her hard.*

*"Joel, oh Joel, oh Joel, pleasseeeee…… fuck me harder…."*
-- Tasha was screaming.

*"I'm on my way, I'm on my way!"*

It took Joel some time to grasp that the second voice was coming from his mother, and he didn't know who it was at first.

Seeing his mother standing only a few feet away stroking her fingers in and out her wet pussy as she stared at his son cock in Tasha's hot cunt made him feel like an **Alpha male**.

I'm fucking your sister with the same wet cock that I fucked you with, Mom.

Honey, go ahead, *fuck her. Fuck her as hard as you can. She needs your huge cock.*

"When it comes to fucking her, the more fucking the better (so that our secret can remain within the three of us), but keep a little juice for me, honey." Ellen said.

Tasha whispered in Joel's ear,

"*Oh, Joel, stop talking and fuck me, fuck me like you will never do again in your lifetime*" as she wrapped her arms around his neck.

"*My feet are not on the ground, so you'll have to do all of the work.*" Tasha also said.

It's not a problem for us, Joel insisted.

His steps were measured, and Tasha's legs were wrapped around his hips as he slowly approached the center-of-the-room game table. He gently placed her back on the cloth-covered surface.

He said, "*Now you are in the perfect place.*"

Again, he slammed into her pussy with a full-force thrust, banging Tasha like he wanted her to pass-out.

With his aunt's pussy covered with fluid, he drew back and rammed his huge cock inside her, over and over again, much harder and faster.

Tasha arched her back in an effort to snag as much cock as she could get her hands on.

*"Joel, fuck me, fuck me, fuck me. I am loving how you are fucking the hell out of my pussy."* Tasha was asking for more!

Now I'm cuming, I am cuming Joel! "

Joel's heart was set off by her scream, and he felt the fluid in his tube finally begin to roll down.

Aunt Tasha, I feel the same way.... *I'm going to shoot your pussy with my cum.*

"Ohhhh. Ooh, that's good." Tasha responded.

When the enormous head spit forth juice, it bathed her pussy walls.

Joel felt like he was going to be pelted with bullets for the rest of his life.

Slushing out of her small hole, some of it ended up pouring down Tasha's backside, as he filled her to the brim with cum.

For Tasha, the thought of a man other than her husband, but her nephew's cum in her pussy was too much to bear, and as another orgasm jellied her insides, she burst into tears.

Joel backed across the room and sat down in his chair as soon as he removed his dripping shaft from her sweet pussy.

His mother (Ellen) sank to her knees and sucked his half-hard penis into her mouth as quickly as she could.

Tasha's legs were dangling lewdly off the table as she lay exhausted.

It's time to stop calling you "*squirt,*" Tasha remarked. I prefer the name "*Alpha - Gusher.*"

*It's like a cascade of your cum pouring out of me. It's a good thing I'm taking that heavy dose of your cum.*

His mother's gaze was fixed on her son's penis, which was reviving itself.

Because I stopped taking the pill three months ago, we may now be referring to him as a father. It hadn't occurred to me that I'd be fucking anyone, not even my own son. But hey, *"it's too late now to be concerned about anything. "* **Ellen** said

*"The only thing I ask is that you both call whenever you want to fuck."* Jokingly, Joel responded.

They (Ellen & Tasha) chanted in unison, *"Count on it!"*

*"What would you do if we were both pregnant? "* Tasha inquired.

Joel gave a sly grin. A second and third set of sisters are waiting for you.

Can you imagine, *"Jeez, listen to him,"* she chuckled. *"Wow."*

She was eventually able to muster the energy to rise to her feet and turn to face Joel.

In response to his mother's head bobbing up and

down, he threw his head back while thrusting his hips forward.

Is Joel really this serious? "*Damn,*" Tasha muttered.

"*You really want to continue fucking,*" she said.

Joel could only nod in agreement.

If only we could fuck and suck together in the same bed.

"*God, wouldn't that be a fun time?*" Joel said.

It took her a moment to come to terms. Her response was to say,

"*I'm all for trying to make it work, and maybe we could even attempt a bigger thing because I'm quite sure she swings both ways.*"

That was the spark that lit the fuse.

To make matters worse, Joel's crotch grew even wider.

Joel screamed, "*Ohh mommmmm, I'm cumming, I'm cumming again.*"

Ellen sank her face into his pubic hair and swallowed his cum, as her mouth and throat were flooded with the scent of his genitals.

**The End!**

Follow my Author profile and connect with me for more exciting ecstatic and romantic erotic stories.

# Thank You!

# Free Bonus

**Grab My "At The Beach (Erotic Romance Story)" Ebook For FREE!**

Today you can grab your copy of my Free Erotic Romance story e-book titled – **At The Beach**. Best of all, it won't cost you a thing.

*Download and Subscribe for Free book, giveaways, and new releases by* **Karena Donger.**

Click the image above to **Download the Book**, and also Subscribe for Free books, giveaways, and new releases by me.

Or Follow the link below;

https://mayobook.com/karenadonger

As my subscriber, you will enjoy more free books exclusive to subscribers only, plus **Free Giveaways**. Wait no further, join my growing number of book lovers, and let's connect.

# About The Author

I'm a romance writer and I've been writing for 10+ years. I write dark and romantic erotica. I have a penchant for romance. I also have a fondness for writing stories that inspire, and a love for the genre of romantic fiction. I write dark and erotic romance because I love the power of darkness and the eroticism that comes with it. I love the passion and the desire. I love the way a man will stop at nothing to get what he wants.

I also write fantasy and contemporary romance because I love the magic and adventure of it, coupled with the modern world and the characters in it. I love the modern family and modern relationships.

I have always loved reading romance novels, and now I am writing them too. I hope to share my love of romance with readers through my writing.

Visit https://mayobook.com/karenadonger to download my Free Erotic story **"At The Beach"** Today!

# Other Books

1. The Road Trip (Mother and Son's Secret Book 1)

2. The Road Trip 2 (Mother and Son's Secret Book 2)

3. Our Secret (Mother and Son's Secret Book 3)

4. Our Secret 2 (Mother and Son's Secret Book 4)

5. The Road Trip Secret, Complete Series Box Set (Mother and Son's Secret)

* 9 7 8 1 6 3 7 5 0 3 0 0 3 *